Yuri Gagarin of the U.S.S.R. became the first man in space on April 12, 1961, in the rocket *Vostok 1*. He circled the earth, and his flight lasted 1 hour 48 minutes.

On May 5, 1961, Alan Shepard became the first American (and second astronaut) to venture into space. His flight in the Mercury capsule *Freedom 7* lasted only 15 minutes.

The first American to orbit the earth was John Glenn, who did so three times in the *Friendship 7* on February 20, 1962. His flight lasted 4 hours 55 minutes.

fuel tank

rocket boosters

The space shuttle *Columbia* first launched into space on April 12, 1981. A shuttle usually stays in orbit for five to ten days and uses rocket boosters to get into space; the boosters are jettisoned along with the fuel tank after its launch.

Paul Collicutt

Farrar Straus Giroux • New York

This book is for my parents, who gave me Neil Armstrong's autograph

Copyright © 2005 by Paul Collicutt
All rights reserved
Distributed in Canada by Douglas & McIntyre Publishing Group
Color separations by Hong Kong Scanner Arts
Printed and bound in the United States of America by Phoenix Color Corporation
Designed by Jay Colvin
First edition, 2005
1 3 5 7 9 10 8 6 4 2

www.fsgkidsbooks.com

Library of Congress Cataloging-in-Publication Data
Collicutt, Paul.
    This rocket / Paul Collicutt.— 1st ed.
        p.   cm.
    ISBN-13: 978-0-374-37484-6
    ISBN-10: 0-374-37484-8
    1. Rockets (Aeronautics)—Juvenile literature.   I. Title.

TL782.5.C56 2005
621.43'56—dc22
                                            2004047059

This rocket lights up the night sky.

This rocket zooms up.

This rocket splashes down.

This rocket has a big astronaut.

This rocket has a small astronaut.

This rocket arrives at the space station.

This rocket leaves the space station.

This rocket is tall.

This rocket is short.

This rocket moves fast.

This rocket is moved slowly.

This rocket is like a car.

This rocket is like a train.

This rocket goes far.

This rocket stays still.

This rocket travels by day.

This rocket travels by night.

This rocket is carried under a plane.

This rocket is carried on top of a truck.

This rocket is being designed.

This rocket is being built.

This rocket is in final countdown:

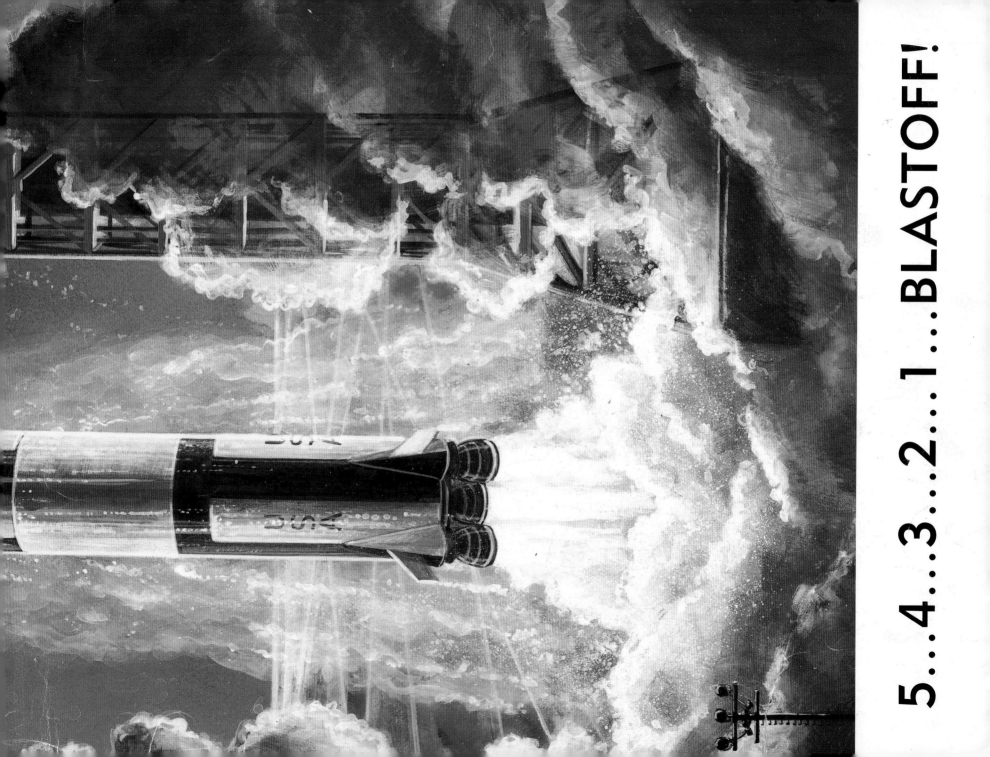

5...4...3...2...1...BLASTOFF!

FLYING TO THE MOON: THE *APOLLO 11* MISSION

The Saturn V rocket—the most powerful rocket ever built—and the *Apollo* spacecraft together stood 363 feet tall.

Launch escape tower

Command module

Service module

Lunar module

Apollo spacecraft

Third stage

Second stage

First stage

Saturn V rocket

USA

3. The launch escape tower and then the second (middle) stage are jettisoned.

2. The first stage (bottom part of the rocket) is jettisoned 2 minutes 42 seconds after liftoff.

4. The Saturn V goes into orbit 9 minutes 15 seconds after liftoff.

1. The Saturn V launches from Earth

6. After leaving orbit, the command/service module pulls out of the third stage, turns around, and docks with the lunar module to form the *Apollo* spacecraft. The third stage is left behind to crash into the moon.

5. The third (top) stage fires up its rocket again and leaves Earth's orbit.

7. The lunar spacecraft is now ready to head for a moon landing.